Reflecting on Moments in Time

A Simple Collection of Rhymes for Everyday Life

Cover design by Becky Benfield-
Humberstone

https://www.fieldandstone.co.uk/

Cover image credit to Roegger on
https://pixabay.com/

Alistair Birch

Introduction

Included within this book are over eighty poems that I have written in the last year or two. Some are plain silly, or I hope at least a little funny. Some are sad whilst others offer empathy for those going through difficult times. Most are suitable for all ages of reader, though a few will have minor cheek.

I hope you will have as much fun reading and sharing them as I did when I wrote them.

Alistair

Contents

7

The Funny Ones

Silly Poems with Animals

Squirrels

I have two squirrels visit,
who think they're at a rave.
I named one squirrel Bob,
the other I call Dave.

This pair of friendly squirrels,
dashing down my tree.
The one who is more friendly,
waves nuts for all to see.

They are pretty funny.
They're dancing all around.
Soon there's other squirrels,
who skip along my ground.

This super squirrel party,
seems to be quite tame,
but then it turned all sinister,
as other squirrels came.

Those who remember Hitchcock,
may remember Birds.
Now my gardens filled,
with lots of squirrel turds.

I shout at them to leave.
'Enough,' I say, 'begone.'
They look at me amused,
and poop another one.

So now I have a problem.
A garden full of poo.
The squirrels are in residence.
I don't know what to do.

Can someone out there,
help me clear them out?
Is there a Pied Piper,
to do a squirrel rout?

At last I found an answer.
It seems they do not like.
When I do karaoke,
and sing into a mic.

The Slug

The slug it moved across the lawn,
with its silvery trail.
Sleek and rather shiny,
but not like any snail.

The children when they saw it,
they squealed and ran away.
Won't touch the slimy creature,
all dark and rather grey.

The gardener didn't like it,
to see the plants, it ate.
Put some pellets on the ground,
he planned to seal its fate.

The slug was rather clever.
He saw the gardeners plan,
and sliding past the pellets laid,
he followed nasty man.

The slug followed to the house,
taking lots of time.
Away from all the poison,
it was doing fine.

Once it got inside,
the slug it felt quite wrecked.
Taking lunch and a nap,
by pot plant he'd inspect.

Before he really knew it,
the sun had gone away.
Snores sounding from above,
signalled end of day.

With quiet determination,
the slug it climbed the stair.
Leaving its silver marker,
across the carpet hair.

The midnight hour it came and went,
the progress it was slow.
The slug it must hurry up,
else dawn light soon would glow.

Eventually amid snoring,
the gardener lay asleep.
Climbing up a bedpost,
the slug began to creep.

Soon upon the pillow,
the slug it moved so near.
The gardener snorted happily,
absent of any fear.

Up over the gardener's chin,
and all across his nose,
a snot like trail was spreading.
The man he suddenly froze.

A cough and sneeze later,
his eyes sprang so wide.
The slug upon his upper lip,
continued onward glide.

Fear and confusion,
filled the gardener's brain.
The sticky nasal residue,
made him feel insane.

Now the slugs plan,
took a nasty route.
The mouth got much wider,
like a rubbish chute.

A second or two later,
down inside it fell.
Tongue and slug combined,
to both it felt like hell.

Eyes wide and choking,
breathing turning slack.
The slug continued downwards,
Then stuck at the back.

So here our tale ends,
and sadly, for these two,
the slug it lay imprisoned,
the gardeners face turned blue.

There is no moral ending,
in this tale of mine,
though if you are quite sensible,
on slugs you shouldn't dine.

Seagulls

I sat upon a deckchair,
to watch the world go by,
when all of a sudden,
a lump fell from the sky.

It wasn't a big snowflake,
though seemed a shade of white.
It was in fact some bird poop,
that gave me quite a fright.

I sat and saw poop falling.
It landed in a clump.
A flock of sea gulls stared at me,
then took another dump.

Now this was getting serious.
I dodged both left and right.
The deckchair bore the brunt,
all flecked in bits of shite.

I ran through the park.
The birds they followed me.
I sped towards a family,
who'd set a picnic tea.

Now, what I did next,
may not sit too well.
I led the seagulls forward.
The picnic went to hell.

How much poop they carry?
I tell you quite a lot.
The family sat in disbelief,
as quickly off I shot.

The bombardment it continued,
the kids began to shout.
The parents flailed their arms about,
but couldn't stop the rout.

The children squinted skyward.
The parents showed despair.
A boy and girl together,
with sticky strands of hair.

When the birds were finished,
with no more poop to drop.
Seagulls swooped in mockery,
above the pooey plop.

The family they were stunned,
and soon began to cry.
The dad looked so miserable,
with poo inside his eye.

If you ever find yourself,
pelted from the sky.
Lead them to target range,
or get into the dry.

Looking from a distance,
I felt a sense of shame.
I'd led all the seagulls,
and I must be to blame.

But then I stopped and caught myself,
it really wasn't me.
It was those pesky seagulls,
who crapped on family tea.

The Fly

The frog it sat upon the pad,
with water all around.
Shooting out a long pink tongue,
at fly on nearby ground.

With froggys tongue a slurping,
the fly it flew away.
Using quick reactions,
to live another day.

Soon the fly it landed,
with eight eyes watching on.
One tiny step closer,
the fly is surely gone.

Sensing some danger,
the fly took to flight.
Spider looked on hungrily,
as dinner flew out of sight.

Needing time to rest,
the fly arrived up high.
Unaware of beady eyes,
swooping from the sky.

A shadow cast upon the branch,
where fly had stopped to wait.
A bird descended quickly,
but it arrived too late.

Thinking it was safer,
outside, upon the ground,
until the mower cut up the grass,
with awful deafening sound.

Feeling rather persecuted,
it buzzed towards a door.
Seeing it was set ajar,
it carried on some more.

Now it found a table,
and settled in the warm.
Surely safe inside the house,
free from any harm.

It wasn't free from danger.
I waved my swatting stick.
It really wasn't quick enough,
to avoid my deftly flick.

Suddenly the fly is squashed,
and I feel no remorse.
Had it been a cat or dog,
I'd think differently of course.

If you are a fly,
buzzing in my flat.
You'd better get right out of there,
or else there'll be a splat.

Bobbie the Rabbit

Bobbie was a rabbit,
who wished that she could fly.
She'd poke out from her hole,
and dream of soaring high.

Foxy saw the rabbit,
and he began to plot.
Picturing fallen Bobbie,
in his cooking pot.

The fox called out to Bobbie,
'If you want to fly.
Climb the nearest mountain,
to get into the sky.'

Bobbie thought a moment.
These words, they were a gift.
Of course, high up a mountain,
she'd get her airborne lift.

Bobbie started marching,
to take the mountain route,
though in all her haste,
she took no parachute.

Away from grassy plains,
she reached the mountain base.
Further back crept Foxy,
a smile upon his face.

Halfway up the mountain,
Bobbie looked about.
She saw the fox beneath her,
and did a little shout.

'Foxy are you following?
Why are you up here?'
Foxy grinned with shining teeth,
'To watch you fly my dear.'

Bobbie thought of flying,
and why she'd climbed up high.
She didn't sense the danger,
all she saw was sky.

Further up the mountain,
Bobbie did a hop.
Foxy always close behind,
to the mountain top.

Above an eagle swooped.
He saw some tasty food.
Foxy saw the eagle,
and he began to brood.

Once atop the mountain,
Bobbie scratched her head.
The sky was still far away.
She stood on rocks instead.

Jumping up frantically,
Bobbie flapped her paws.
Landing with a bump,
she spied some eagle claws.

The eagle hurtled downward,
and Foxy onward raced.
Bobbie realised way too late,
the peril she now faced.

The eagle grabbed poor Bobbie,
and Foxy grabbed her too.
Soon the mountain fell away,
as off the threesome flew.

Now the things went badly,
as three began to fall.
Eagle knew he'd hold just one,
but could not carry all.

Foxy held on in panic,
and Bobbie felt his grip.
Eagle clutching rabbit,
and hoping fox would slip.

Alas they held together,
and fell to valley floor.
Crumpled fur and feathers,
of three that were so sore.

Once the dust had settled,
Bobbie took a look.
Nearby was her burrow,
so, at speed she took.

Foxy was all dazed,
and he just slunk away.
Eagle flew up the mountain,
to search for other prey.

Bobbie learned her lesson,
she stopped her plans to fly.
She searched for a new hobby,
that she would like to try.

She settled upon diving,
and hoped to swim the sea.
To find out what happened,
you'll have to wait and see.

Bobbie the Rabbit - Part Two

Bobbie was a rabbit,
and once she had a dream.
It all went really badly,
and caused her quite a scream.

After flying was so scary,
you'd think she'd take a rest,
but Bobbie didn't give up,
and sought a new interest.

Bobbie fancied swimming.
She hoped that one day,
to find a sea to swim in,
but this was miles away,

She went to a road,
to try and hitch a ride,
but all the cars ignored her,
and left her on the side.

Then one lorry stopped,
and Bobbie hopped right in.
She didn't see the butchers sign,
or sneaky drivers grin.

As they drove on forwards,
they found a meat factory.
Bobbies eyes widened,
as this was not the sea.

The driver went to grab her,
hungry for some tea.
Bobbie leapt out the window,
or in a pie she'd be.

Bobbie was determined.
The sea still called to her.
She bounded out the door,
a speedy ball of fur.

Eventually she arrived,
at a sandy beach.
She wanted scuba gear,
but this was out of reach.

Tired and defeated,
she set her dream aside.
The water lapped beyond her,
receding with the tide.

Now if she'd ventured further,
to water she'd descend,
the sharks would have eaten her,
and that would be the end.

But I am here quite happily,
to tell you she's ok.
Bobbie made it home,
to live another day.

The Frog

There was a frog,
sat on a log,
in the midday sun.
A girl came by,
with lazy eye,
and thought she'd have some fun.

Sat on the log,
beside the frog,
she offered up a kiss.
The frog said croak,
as though a joke,
then made a noisy hiss.

She had a think,
then gave a wink,
but froggy didn't budge.
Again, a pout,
beneath her snout,
then gave the frog a nudge.

The frog cast eye,
and wondered why,
the girl would want a snog.
She looked up
and puckered up,
to try and kiss the frog.

The lips were set
and then they met,
as girl and froggy kissed.
But froggy slime,
was not sublime,
and now she wished she'd missed.

Her eyes were wide,
the girl she cried,
'you are not a prince.'
She felt sick,
the girl so thick,
though gave her mouth a rinse.

The moral here,
is very clear.
A frog is just a frog.
If you or me,
see a frog or three,
leave them on their log.

I Have a Little Dragon

I have a little dragon,
who sleeps just next to me.
She is rather awesome,
though snores quite noisily.

Now my little dragon,
She's cute and she is kind.
She doesn't know she's snoring.
She doesn't seem to mind.

Often, she is fast asleep,
as I lay wide awake.
I look on quite lovingly,
despite a noisy quake.

The snoring doesn't matter,
as I am truly blessed.
I hug my little dragon,
in her little nest.

Would I change my dragon?
No way I ever would.
I love my snoring dragon,
in every way I should.

And if you have a dragon,
who keeps you up at night.
Love your little dragon,
and always hold it tight.

The Rolling Aardvark

Annie was an Aardvark,
who rolled into a ball,
across the bedroom carpet,
and out into the hall.

Bouncing down the stairs,
she rolled right through a door,
hitting a poor postman,
who fell down to the floor.

Postie yelled angrily,
'Oi what's your game?'
Annie kept on rolling,
along and down the lane.

She came to a crossing.
'Stop' the sign it said.
She kept her momentum,
the cars they bumped instead.

Twisted metal and carnage,
Annie left behind.
Blissful in her ignorance,
she didn't seem to mind.

Then at last she reached it,
though hill was far too steep.
Annie started forwards,
then came backward creep.

Annie didn't like this,
the backward rolling run.
Returning her once more,
to where she had just come.

Back towards the drivers,
howling at their wrecks.
Back towards the postie,
who said, 'What the heck?'

At last our rolling Aardvark,
was back inside the home.
The front door slamming shut,
preventing further roam.

So, if you see an Aardvark,
rolling in the street.
Ask if it is Annie,
she's really rather sweet.

Nursery Rhymes and old Stories

Not The Three Little Pigs

Have you heard the tale,
of pigs, one two three?
Told to all the children,
snuggled after tea.

One built a house of straw,
and one had house of sticks,
then there was the wolf,
who couldn't blow the bricks.

What I shall tell you,
may come as a surprise.
This is not what happened.
In fact, it may be lies.

Now if you don't like grisly,
bin this rhyme quite quick.
Do not read much further,
or risk you will be sick.

For this different version,
picture in your mind,
first pig, I'll call him Percy,
all charitable and kind.

Porky the younger brother,
he was good and pure.
Lastly there was Pinkie,
who held the most allure.

They went to build their houses,
but along came snotty man,
waving a big clipboard,
from his council van.

'You cannot build your houses,
not without the form.
Get yourselves permission,
or else I'll cause a storm.'

'We're scared the wolf will eat us.
Don't you understand?
Please just let us build,
our houses on this land.'

The council man, he sneered,
determined he would win,
Percy pushed a cement mixer,
and watched the man fall in.

He shrieked and he wailed,
'Please, set me free.
I'll let you build your houses,
for piggy's, one two three.

The pigs they considered this,
and went to let him out,
when stupidly the council man,
let rip a threatening shout.

Pinkie pushed the on switch,
and Porky watched it spin.
The man was ground to powder,
he didn't get his win.

The pigs they set to building.
One house for them all,
with its hidden secret,
underneath the wall.

In an odd circumstance,
the council never checked,
what happened to their man,
they'd sent down to object.

And last of all, the wolf you ask,
well he had gone away.
He'd seen the concrete mixer,
and booked a holiday.

So, if you meet three pigs,
all kind and worth a mention.
Don't try to threaten them,
or you'll become an extension

Goldilocks – Maybe?

Goldilocks,
as most recall,
a greedy girl,
who took it all,
but what if she,
was nice and sweet,
and when she sat,
she meant to eat,
all the junk,
that bears don't like,
when she was out,
on morning hike.
Perhaps indeed,
she did intend,
to be a golden,
kind bear friend.
All the things,
they said she did,
like breaking chairs,
before she hid,
in bed upstairs,
out of view.
All made up.
Were they untrue?
But what of bears,
within that home?
Surely woods are,
where they roam.
Now that I,
have taken time,
I think the bears,

were out of line,
and Goldie with,
the story told,
really had,
a heart of gold.
Bears we know,
are rather wild,
so don't berate,
our golden child,
and if you see,
a bear, or three.
Don't invite,
them in for tea.

An Alternative Christmas Carol

A Christmas Carol by Dickens,
is a masterpiece we know.
Here is my disclaimer,
for all the words below.

Every word I've written here,
is make believe and fake.
No comparison to Dickens work,
should anyone ever make.

In the original novel,
was Ebenezer Scrooge.
But in my silly poem,
is Eddie 'The Squeezer' Snooze.

Now Eddie was a wrestler,
who crushed the others tight,
but then one day it went away,
as he lost every fight.

Giving up the wrestling,
he took his business brain,
and bought an accounting company,
though each bill looked the same.

But accountancy it bored him.
His will began to lose.
Very soon the staff could see,
all he did was snooze.

The workers they were restless,
for all them worked so hard,
but despite all their efforts,
no pay rise on the card.

One day Eddie's partner,
left and went away.
Jacob Harley Farley,
gone in mysterious way.

As Christmas came around,
the staff deserved a break,
but Eddie wouldn't countenance,
the mean and vicious snake.

On Christmas Eve, the workers,
hoped the day would end.
Horrible boss old Eddie,
off home he wouldn't send.
Finally, so late,
they were allowed to go.
Trudging off in misery,
through deep and chilling snow.

'Be back at work tomorrow,
and don't try anything cute.'
The workers turned and faced him,
to wave two fingered salute.

With all the staff departed,
Eddie went to bed,
but Jacob Harley Farley,
stared at him instead.

'Why on earth are you here?'
He used another word.
'I am here to warn you,
you stupid useless turd.'

'You are really nasty,
and threat your staff so shite.
Be much better to them all,
starting from tonight.'

And then a moment later,
the room was dark and still.
Eddie farted loudly,
and took a sleeping pill.

It seemed a mere moment,
but the room began to shake.
'I am the ghost of Christmas past,
now rouse yourself awake.'

Eddie looked up blinking.
Who disturbed his sleep?
Was it Harley Farley,
the stupid little creep?

'Look at these memories,
of how you used to be.
Dropped you down upon your head,
and turned you bad you see.'

'Before you were a wrestler,
you were fairly kind.
Then you got all bashed about,
and clearly lost your mind.'

Now I'm not saying wrestling,
will turn them all so dark,
but all of that pounding,
is sure to leave a mark.

The ghost flew through a window,
according to some accounts,
leaving a weird smell,
just like Brussels sprouts.

Disturbed and getting angry,
with his lack of sleep.
He pulled apart the curtains,
and took a little peep.

Out in the street below,
snow was laying thick,
but heading for his window,
another ghost came quick.

Now Eddie wasn't frightened,
indeed, felt quite tough.
This new ghost wasn't welcome.
Now he'd had enough.

The third ghost it ignored him,
and swept onto the bed.
Eddie flailed at the cloudy lump,
and punched himself instead.

Ignoring stunned Eddie,
and with a squeaky voice.
'Look at you, all alone,
there is another choice.'

Again, this ghost it vanished,
and left old Ed confused.
Switching on the bedside lamp,
he found a mighty bruise.

Sitting on the bed,
he wished that sleep would come,
instead he heard chains rattling,
and this time he said 'Mum?'

Another ghost appeared,
and this was tall and loud.
Wrapped up poor old Eddie,
within an icy shroud.

The room it spun quite quickly,
and then it was no more.
Eddie felt quite fearful,
And sought the exit door.

No doors were laid before him.
All was empty space.
Eddie stared at nothingness.
What was this awful place?

'Total isolation,'
the ghost it said to him,
'This is where you're headed,
so, take it on the chin.'

'But this can't be,' said Eddie,
'I'll be nice again.'
'Don't put me here, for I do fear,
that I will go insane.'

Now in the Dickens story,
everything was alright,
as Scrooge he turned a corner.
He really saw the light.

Sadly, in this version,
there is no happy end.
Eddie couldn't change.
His ways he didn't mend.

Now if you've just read this.
Do not feel too sad.
Unless your name is Eddie,
and you've been rather bad.

The Ogre

I know you're told the tale,
of billy goats who were gruff.
In fact you're probably fed up.
You may have heard enough.

The problem with the ogre,
we misunderstood.
In fact he was quite kindly,
and really rather good.

The ogre he had battled,
and fought for queen and crown,
then returned to his homeland,
to try and settle down.

He wasn't really an ogre,
but war had left him scared.
Now many they derided him,
no fairness in reward.

The ogre he was damaged,
by all he'd seen and done.
Needed care and understanding,
but sadly there was none.

The first goat in this story,
was just like you or me.
An ordinary citizen,
like many that we see.

Underneath a bridge,
our ogre lay all cold.
First goat stepped away from him,
like he was made of mould.

The second goat held status,
in the local town,
but she moved the ogre on,
with a dreadful frown.

The last goat he had influence,
elected with our votes.
He cut the welfare spending,
and dashed our ogres hopes.

In the first storytelling,
ogre was tossed away.
Down into the river,
lost this very day.

Now if you meet an ogre,
keep an open mind.
They may be very worthy,
so make sure you are kind.

Cinderella - An Alternative Version

With panto season near us,
I thought I'd share with you.
An often-spoken story,
set upon a skew.

The tale of Cinderella,
is one we know quite well.
Stepsisters so ugly,
and a step mum right from hell.

But did you ever realise,
that maybe things weren't right.
The stepfamily wasn't all that bad,
and Cinders was the fright.

The person who told the story,
was Cinders, so you see.
She changed the story round about,
and lied to you and me.

I have it on good authority,
that what I write is true.
Cinders was a nasty cow,
who often smelt of poo.

Cinders real mother,
a lady known as Belle,
she had a rather sticky end,
shoved inside a well.

Her father was so mortified.
His wife was sadly dead.
Cinders rubbed onion in her face,
To make her eyes most red.

More than one year later,
Cinders ruled the roost.
Father found a new wife,
which gave him quite a boost.

Together with a new mum,
two sisters came as well.
All with grace, and pretty of face,
who really didn't smell.

Cinders didn't like this,
she saw her power lost.
She plotted through gritted teeth,
to rid them at all cost.

One day the prince announced,
a ball for all the town.
Girls filled with excitement,
each shopping for a gown.

Now we believe that Cinders,
was the one who cleaned the fire.
In reality she did no jobs,
and this was getting dire.

Now the next bit is a quite grizzly,
so younger ones don't read.
Stepsister Drizella,
was turned to animal feed.

Following straight after,
stepsister number two,
Anastasia had a similar fate,
as poison turned her blue.

Her stepmother became quite frantic,
two daughters out of sight.
She thought Cinders had done them in.
You know I think she might.

Picking up her things,
step mum she crept away.
She would be dead as well,
if she stayed another day.

By now her dad had seen enough,
though fearing for his life.
He packed a bag, full of stuff,
and ran after his wife.

With all her competition vanquished,
Cinders dressed quite smart.
Though nobody dared to say,
she really looked a tart.

In the story you all know,
with fairy godmother spark,
but magic is just nonsense,
and shoes came from Primark.

With no Fairy Godmother,
there was no pumpkin coach.
So, Cinders called an Uber,
and the ball she did approach.
At the Ball, Prince Charming,
entertained all with pride.
Cinders found her slippers of glass,
were made to slip and slide.

Slowly people noticed,
and they began to snort.
All of Cinders wooing plans,
blew up before the court.

So even though Cinders,
wasn't a royal heir.
She wrote words you know,
and plastered it everywhere.

All can choose their ending,
that they will read this week.
Sparkly happy endings,
or lots of tongue in cheek.

Hansel & Gretel - An Alternative Version

Hansel & Gretel, is a story,
That you may have read.
Did you hear the version,
where they were bad instead?

They wouldn't do their homework,
their bedrooms were a mess.
Always they were lazy,
with father in distress.

'Please do some washing up',
he asked after tea?
'You can stick your dishes,'
they both said gleefully.

'Time for bed you children,
it's getting rather late.'
Our naughty pair ignored him,
and walked out through the gate.

'Let's go out and party,'
said Gretel with a sneer.
'Will the pub serve us,
if we go for a beer?'

Thinking they'd be lucky,
to get a glass of ale,
they wandered through the forest,
and left a rubbish trail.

Hearing lots of animals,
they picked up lots of stones.
Threw them at the shadows,
to hope to break some bones.

A screech behind the bushes,
made the children grin.
They hoped to hurt an animal.
Caring not for sin.

Beyond the darkened bushes,
lay a lady in the dirt.
She was very upset.
Clearly, she was hurt.

Not caring that they'd hit her,
the pair they ran away.
Both were laughing loudly,
leaving such dismay.

The path became much thinner,
as light began to fade.
Slowly the naughty children,
remembered beds unmade.

Their house it was so warm,
away from evening chill.
Now the looming shadows,
took away their thrill.

Walking in a circle,
the pair were truly lost.
They stumbled to a cottage,
with walls of icing frost.

Feeling really greedy,
the pair began to eat.
Damaging the building,
To take their sugar treat.

They munched at a windowsill,
until a pane it fell.
Suddenly in the darkness,
there came an awful yell.

Seeing they'd been rumbled,
the pair looked to run,
but legs were all knotted,
with lots of chewing gum.

Staring through the hole,
where the window used to be,
was the forest lady,
with bruises, one, two, three.

Now I'm sure you expect,
To have a happy end.
The children will apologise,
and somehow make amend.

But sadly, this didn't happen,
and with this grisly tale,
the woman was a witch,
with powers she'd avail.

She took the naughty children,
and dumped them in her pot.
Stewed them with some sugar,
to patch the wall a lot.

Other Silly Ones

Gordon the Goblin

Gordon was a Goblin.
He did what Goblins do.
Hiding in the woods,
scaring me and you.

Nearing Halloween,
he rubbed his hands with glee.
Thought he'd steal the sweeties,
meant for you and me.

The children dressed as monsters,
went from door to door.
Gordon in the shadows,
hid upon the floor.

A girl dressed as a mummy,
with bandage covered eye.
Stood on naughty Gordon,
then kicked him in the thigh.

Then came several ghouls,
dripping lots of slime.
Gordon's face got plastered,
he didn't move in time.

Along came a werewolf,
waving mighty claw.
Scratching in the darkness,
caught Gordon on the jaw.

Suddenly there's Dracula,
wielding pointy stake,
whacked Gordon's kneecaps,
and almost made them break.

Frankenstein's monster,
stomped across the room.
Clumpy boots were trampling.
Gordon filled with gloom.

Gordon sloped off home,
feeling very glum.
The children they were monsters,
each and every one.

The kids they got their sweeties,
and Gordon went to bed.
He wouldn't be stealing anything,
but went to sleep instead.

If you plan on thieving,
think what happened here.
Don't be a naughty goblin.
Stay in and drink a beer.

Dinner

As Jimmy came back home from school,
he asked his mum for tea.
'Stupid boy, your older now,
you should cook for me. '

Jimmy wondered for a bit,
if he had heard quite right.
Cooking isn't easy,
and gave him quite a fright.

'But mum he said quite meekly,
I don't know what to do.
I can't think of what to cook,
to eat for me and you.'

Mothers red eyes widened,
she stood up tall and straight.
'I am really hungry.
Do not make me wait.'

'Make me roast beef dinner,
and cook it really quick.
I have hardly eaten,
and starving makes me sick. '

Looking in the fridge,
there was no beef in sight,
Jimmy wondered what to do,
to feed his mum that night.

'I cannot find the beef.'
Jimmy told his mum.
Angrily, she replied,
'Are you really dumb?'

'I am your mother,
and I gave birth to you.
I demand you feed me,
my food is overdue.'

The cupboards they were empty.
He really couldn't win.
Getting really worried now,
he looked within the bin.

Seeing there was lettuce,
and beans and bits of rice,
Jimmy kept on searching,
for something really nice.

Delving a little deeper,
buried out of sight,
sat half a tin of cat food,
gleaming in the light.

In a thrice, he grabbed the rice,
and scooped the cat food too,
popped it all in a pot,
with apple core and glue.

Soon the pot was bubbling,
giving it a stir.
Carpet fluff and lots of stuff,
hoping mum would purr.

'Where is my dinner?
Why do you make me wait?
Am I worth so little to you,
to make my meal so late?'

At last the food was on a plate,
all hot and full of spice.
Mum sat down, without a frown,
and suddenly seemed nice.

Scoffing down her dinner,
mum was lost for words,
as the glue took effect,
and gummed her vocal cords.

As he sat and watched her,
he wondered what to do.
Should he try to help her,
to free her from the glue?

She sat there very quietly,
mouth all taut and tight.
Lips were locked quite solidly,
though eyes were deadly bright.

In this little story,
the mum was rather mean.
All very demanding,
a right drama queen.

If you are a parent,
who is just much too tough.
You can choose, to not abuse,
or things may end quite rough.

If you are a child,
and mum is kind and fair.
Do some jobs around the house,
and help her everywhere.

The moral of this story?
Do ask but be quite kind,
or like this mum, here today,
could end in a bind.

A Week of Mishaps

When I was rather young,
I was taught out loud.
If the game was over,
toss the ball into the crowd.

Now I am thinking,
maybe that was wrong.
The bowling club have banned me,
like I do not belong.

The next day, off I walked,
with my lovely dog.
We found ourselves a beach,
I even did a jog.

It looks once again,
wrong I seemed to be.
Calling my dog 'Shark',
caused calamity.

My week was going badly,
but Wednesday started well,
working in a bakery,
with cakes that we could sell.

I knew what I was doing,
I felt confident.
I collected lots of pebbles,
for rock cakes like cement.

Sacked from the bakery,
my mood it turned quite low.
Everyone who spoke to me,
called me rather slow.

Next job as a carpet fitter,
ended in short while.
I lost the family hamster.
Gone beneath the pile.

All of these failings,
ground me down inside.
I searched for a job,
that I could do with pride.

I put my pen to paper,
and wrote a line or two.
Suddenly I'm a poet,
writing rhymes for you.

The moral of this story.
Even if you fail,
pick yourself back up,
until you can prevail.

The Giggle

I just want to giggle,
as something tickled me.
I love to laugh at jokes,
and humour that I see.

When I laugh, I notice,
that people may laugh too.
I'll pass my giggle onward.
A gift from me to you.

Now we're both laughing,
although a little loud.
Soon we hear some others,
become a giggle crowd.

Chuckles they are flowing,
though most they know not why.
This giggling's infectious,
it makes us want to cry.

Life filled with laughter,
is living at its best.
So, spend you day laughing,
and share your happiness.

The Teapot

I came across a teapot,
with very tiny spout.
I went to pour my drink,
but heard a little shout.

Looking down inside,
everything was dark,
but as I pulled the lid,
out shot a tiny spark.

My head it fell backward.
This came as a surprise.
Staring up from inside,
a girl with hairy thighs.

I know what you are thinking,
a girl with hairy thighs?
It is most odd, the hairy sod,
though she had lovely eyes.

I wondered what to do.
Should I seal the lid?
I spoke rather gently,
and out the pot she slid.

Sitting on the table,
I saw her hairy legs.
It left me rather curious,
or was it tea leaf dregs?

Who on earth are you,
and why sit in the pot?
Weren't you boiled up,
when sat in water hot?

She sat and she stared at me,
before she did reply.
She only said one word,
and that was just 'Goodbye'

She dived in the pot again,
and suddenly was gone.
I looked within the darkness,
though lost was everyone.

Sat at the table,
I drank my cup of tea,
and wondered what I'd seen,
an odd reality.

Maybe I was drunk.
Had someone spiked my drink?
I took a little pause,
to really stop and think.

I'm hoping I was dreaming.
Was it in my head?
Am I'm going mad?
Should I go to bed?

Now if it really happened,
and my brain is fried.
You have my permission,
to have me certified.

Itching

I'm itching, I'm twitching,
an itch upon my arm.
If I brush against you,
will you come to harm?

You're itching, you're twitching,
itch is on your head.
Now you touch someone else,
so, they can itch instead.

He's itching, he's twitching,
now it's on his neck.
Leaning in towards someone,
he tries to plant a peck.

She's itching, she's twitching,
now it's on her chest.
She seems to be complaining,
'It's like a nylon vest.'

We're itching, we're twitching,
creating quite a scene.
Now we're all together,
sat in quarantine.

The Fart Poem

Yuck, that stink.
What have done to me?
Did you just fart?
What did you eat for tea?

Yes, my dear,
I really think I must.
It's the cabbage I just ate.
Now you look concussed.

I'm wafting, I'm waving.
Your pong it fills the room.
Your bum is like a chem lab,
dumping toxic gloom.

Please, don't say,
you've done another one.
My eyes are weeping,
from your smelly bomb.

I can't stand it.
I've really had enough.
Need to step outside,
to stop me feeling rough.

You just sit there,
smiling broad and wide,
looking so innocent,
though giggles are inside.

Why must you laugh,
at all your silent pong.
I prefer the noisy ones.
Stinky is so wrong.

Can I forgive you,
for what you did to me?
Go off to the kitchen,
and make a cup of tea.

While you are up there,
put cabbage in the bin.
Unless it's in coleslaw,
it causes gassy sin.

The Angry Granny

(Warning, this one is a little bit cheekier)

Mildred was a granny,
her kindness oft did show.
Smiling at the animals,
and folks that you may know.

She always was so peaceful,
in her neighbourhood.
Quiet and contented,
things that are so good.

But Mildred had a secret.
At night when things got dark,
she took a walk with paint ball gun,
to hide within the park.

She waited by the slide.
She stood behind the trees.
She hid under the bushes,
and hoped she wouldn't sneeze.

The kids who lived close by to her,
thought that they were tough.
They were bullies, one and all,
who like to play too rough.

These adolescents,
were rotten, through and through.
Mildred set to scare them,
and fill their pants with poo.

Six of them walked along,
kicking broken glass.
She lined her gun up at them,
and shot one in the ass.

The youth yelped, and hopped about,
trousers round his knees.
Look, I've been bloody stung.
Check it will you please?

The others stood agape,
then shared a nasty sneer.
Laughing at their silly friend,
they kicked him in the rear.

Mildred quietly chuckled,
then lined another shot.
Aiming for the tallest youth,
whose face was filled with snot.

He fell back and with a yelp,
clutched his injured leg.
In truth it hit much higher,
and caught his middle peg.

Red paint balls they were fired,
and in a lack of light,
the yobs howled in anguish,
at the scary sight.

The four who still were standing,
seemed to be confused.
Two were sobbing on the floor,
each with purple bruise.

Looking all about them,
seeking out the source.
Fists were raised up high,
in ready show of force.

Now granny was a crack shot,
and once again let fly.
Catching third yob you know where,
sending tears to his eye.

Three, they were rolling,
calling out for mum.
The others went and scattered,
in pandemonium.

I don't advocate violence,
or what this granny did.
I am however glad,
they slunk away and hid.

The neighbourhood was safer,
and folks were out again.
Feeling safe surroundings,
threats were on the wane.

As for those poor boys,
victims some would say.
When they finally stepped out,
Timid was their way.

A vigilante granny,
is a bad idea.
I hope we learn to live,
with kindness, not with fear.

I Love the English Language

Is there a bare bear,
sitting in the woods?
Maybe there are eight who ate,
scoffing all the goods.

Have you ever read the red,
words upon a page?
Did you see a knight at night,
who stood upon a stage?

Do we have some dew due,
early in the morn?
Are we right to write,
even when we yawn.

Where do we wear,
a top that we have bought?
Do you confuse a barrister,
if barista's what you sought?

The thing with English language,
others may find weird.
We have lots of rules.
Not all is as appeared.

'Gh' gives an 'Eff' sound,
if cough's the word we choose,
or 'Gh' sounds like 'Ow',
when bough's the word we use.

'Si' might be for P,
if psyche is our word,
pronouncing 'Che' as 'Key'
seems a bit absurd.

We have our silent letters,
like K when we knock,
or quiet C in a muscle,
but heard in every sock.

Then we've pinched some words,
from countries all around.
Have you ever noticed,
where cul-de-sac is found?

So are there grammar police,
sitting next to you?
Who when they see, 'Their, their,'
turn a shade of blue.

I know that I am human,
whose grammar can be bad,
but I love my English language,
with words that make me glad.

Our American Friends

We had two lovely visitors,
from the USA.
Came to stay one summer,
it really made each day.

But chat was very confusing,
and they were often blank.
We used the Queen's English,
and they spoke English 'Yank'.

Early in the visit,
he asked if we'd a Jon.
'Why yes, he was my uncle,
sadly, now he's gone.'

It was on the next day,
they asked to see a store.
I took them to the garden shed,
and confused them even more.

We went down to the High Street,
he said, 'See that hood.'
I offered him my raincoat,
in case there was a flood.

After we'd been shopping,
I said, 'Please load the boot.'
She filled her Ugg's with lots of sweets,
it really was a hoot.

Then we got quite hungry.
They asked us for some chips.
I gave them each a battered sausage,
which sent them into fits.

After lunch was eaten,
they said they'd need a bar.
Off we went to a builders yard,
driving in my car.

That evening we were chatting,
and 'Sneakers' is what I heard.
Maybe they mean a burglar,
all else would be absurd.

For breakfast on the next day,
'Jelly please,' they chimed.
Served it with some ice cream.
They didn't seem to mind.

Then one sunny day,
they asked about a yard.
'It's slightly shorter than a metre,
it really isn't hard.'

As the trip was nearly done,
she said, 'Nearly fall.'
I grabbed an arm to steady her,
before she hit a wall.

Driving to the airport,
he asked about the gas?
I passed him a Gaviscon,
and let the comment pass.

Now even though they've left us,
and may have flown away.
We love our American cousins.
Come back another day.

The Supermarket

'Unexpected item',
the modern shoppers call.
Looking in my carrier,
there's nothing there at all.

I lift off my bag,
to try and start again.
Tell myself a prayer,
though this is all in vain.

First item scanned.
I think it may be good.
Bleeping out again,
just where I am stood.

Waiting for assistance,
under flashing light.
Why do I feel bad,
when their tech isn't right?

People stood behind me,
annoyed they have to wait.
Others in self-service,
who suffer the same fate.

At last staff come,
to fix their techie bug,
then suddenly they've gone,
with just a simple a shrug.

Another item scanned,
I hope to soon be done,
but sadly, I am wrong,
this test has just begun.

More bleeps at my shopping,
I lift it out and check.
The machine it just mocks me,
with auto 'what the heck.'

Again, the assistant,
slowly wanders by,
keys in a code,
and leaves with just a sigh.

Finally, I'm leaving,
at a hasty trot.
Outside it dawns on me,
the items I forgot.

Shall I return?
Will a queue be free?
Alas I am giving up.
Chippy for our tea.

DNA

What would you do,
if you changed your DNA?
Could you grow some wings?
Would you fly away?

How about eyes,
that saw through everything?
Would that make you happy?
Could it be your thing?

Maybe you'd like super speed,
to whizz along a track.
Running further faster,
and not be at the back.

Would you like telepathy,
to read another's mind?
How would you feel after,
the secrets you may find?

Now if I could do this.
If I had a choice.
I would stay as I am.
Don't need another voice.

I don't seek immortality.
I'll just live my life.
I'll try to be a good father,
and give love to my wife.

Directions

I saw a big old signpost,
as I walked along the road.
On the ground, staring up,
there sat a bulbous toad.

Sticking out its tongue,
it seemed to point me left.
But turning off the road I'm on,
would leave me quite bereft.

I carried straight along,
and ignored a booming croak.
Was the toad instructing me,
or was it all a joke?

Next appeared a river,
with bridge that went across.
A heron stood with beady eye.
It really seemed quite cross.

Seeing I was nearing,
the bird stuck out it's beak.
Pointed it along the bank,
and made a horrid shriek.

I ignored the noisy heron,
and crossed the bridge of brick,
though as I reached the middle,
I'm sure it called me thick.

Straight ahead I carried on,
until I saw a bin.
Big ears, a tail and whiskers,
a rat that seemed quite thin.

The tail it was pointed,
off and too my right.
Ignoring the clear signal,
I soon was out of sight.

The path passed through a field,
with an old oak tree.
Upon a branch, there stood a crow,
staring back at me.

Its beak was hard and yellow,
and seemed to show the way.
I paused at the tree trunk,
In warmth of sunny day.

The crow it seemed annoyed with this,
and let out mighty 'Caw'.
I shrugged my shoulders gently,
to continue on some more.

Soon my home was nearby.
I thought of all I'd heard.
Lots of animals directing me.
I felt it was absurd.

Now I'm back within my home,
my imagination is reset.
No such thing as talking animals,
unless it is your pet.

For as I see the kitchen,
a cat meows at me.
It makes a lot of noise,
impatient for its tea.

After Easter

Easter it has been and gone,
bunny's in its hutch.
Kids ate all the Easter eggs,
they didn't leave too much.

They scoffed the eggs of chocolate,
left wrappers on the floor.
After stuffing faces,
would they ask for more?

When all the choc was eaten,
they slumped with lots of bloat.
Attempts to get them outside,
they wouldn't grab a coat.

Later I gave them veggies,
suddenly they're full.
If it isn't made of choc,
then it's really rather dull.

Do they get the symbolism,
that Easter's all about?
Sadly, they choose indulgence,
and opt to laze about.

Life and Other Stuff

Time Machine

If you built a time machine,
what would you change?
Who could you visit?
Should you rearrange?

Would you try to find me,
when I was quite young?
Would we still be friends?
Would I still belong?

Then there are the bad things.
Dare you interfere?
If you really did,
who would disappear?

Can you use your knowledge,
to help mankind along,
or would you bet the winners,
which sounds kind of wrong.

Maybe all the past has gone.
The futures where it's at.
Stuff to come's exciting.
Did you think of that?

But what if in the future,
humanity is extinct.
Polluters and the greedy,
who didn't stop and think.

I'm not sure I'm ready,
to see that future yet,
and as for time before,
I'd like it to stay set.

For if I changed my history,
to take away the bad,
then despite best intentions,
I'd also lose some glad.

If I Could be a Doctor

If I could be a doctor,
what would I be?
Maybe general practice.
Is that the path for me?

Could I be a surgeon,
and cut you with a knife?
Take away that nasty growth
and hope to save your life.

Then there's cardiology.
I'd listen to your heart,
or gastroenterology,
though that may cause a fart.

What about physiotherapy?
I'd help you get strength back,
then set you on some weights,
or round a running track.

Now there's gynaecology.
Not sure I'd be good.
The ladies all would run away,
and leave me where I'm stood.

Could I do neurology,
and touch a nerve or two,
or could do paediatrics,
with young ones coming through?

Maybe a psychiatrist?
I'd ask about your mum,
and look at your behaviour,
like why you suck your thumb.

In truth there are so many paths,
and I'm not a doctor yet.
I think I prefer animals.
Perhaps I'll be a vet.

Marmite

I love marmite,
thought it's not for some.
Spread the stuff on my toast,
then put it in my tum.

If you do not like it,
that's ok with me.
Eat some jam or honey,
to have instead for tea.

You may think this poem's,
about a yeasty spread.
After all the words above,
are those that you just read.

All I have written,
describes who we meet.
All that diversity,
on each and every street.

We are all so different,
from short through to tall.
Some could be as giants,
others really small.

It doesn't matter to me,
if you are black or white.
Though I prefer those people,
who try to be polite.

I don't mind which country,
where you once were born.
Your culture it is interesting,
never ever worn.

Having faith and love,
for religions that you choose.
Practice beliefs peacefully,
and we shall never lose.

It doesn't matter to me,
if you're gay, bi or straight.
You may be quite different,
but we don't have to mate.

I know a poem like this,
can divide the crowd.
Some find it distasteful,
others may be wowed.

Whether you like marmite,
or it makes you sick.
Tolerance and kindness,
can make a good world tick.

Chatterbox

Polly was a chatterbox,
who really was too loud.
You could hear her far away,
even in a crowd.

Her friends tried to tell her,
'Polly, please be quiet,'
but Polly just spoke over them,
as though it was a riot.

They couldn't get a word in.
It really was a pain.
It was getting just too much,
this ever-noisy game.

Everyone had headaches.
They couldn't make her stop.
Polly cranked her volume,
and dialled it to the top.

They took her to a library,
but all she did was yell.
The librarian, took offence,
and then she did expel.

The cinema was worse.
Before first trailer play.
An angry mob of punters,
wouldn't let them stay.

Should they try to gag her?
Did she have a mute?
Should they drive her far away,
and lock her in the boot?

Of course they didn't do that,
for that would be quite wrong,
but still their ears assaulted,
as Polly switched to song.

One lucky day at market,
they set her up a stall.
Now Polly she is happy,
to shout at one and all.

When the day is ending,
she's loud for many hours.
Polly's voice is quieter,
and we can all hear ours.

So if you are the noisy one,
who won't let friends be heard.
Don't be like Polly was.
That silly noisy bird.

Apologies to all the lovely ladies called Polly
out there.

The Hoarder

I once saw some clutter,
which caused me shock and awe.
The stuff it lay most everywhere,
to me a real eyesore.

'Why do you keep all this,
I really want to know?'
'These are my memories.
Look here, I will show.'

We went into the living room,
and there upon the floor,
stood piles of books and magazines,
that almost blocked the door.

Once I looked much closer,
it wasn't really tat.
Lots of things with sentiment,
more than this or that.

Everything was ordered,
in lines from A to Z.
Seeing all the stories,
waiting to be read.

Moving through the house,
a pattern seemed to form.
Lots of bits and pieces,
that seemed to be the norm.

Although the house was full.
To some it looked a bin.
I could see some character,
a house that was lived in.

'So what will you do,
if you get some more?'
Came a reply so simple,
'Oh I have got a store.'

I quite enjoyed my visit,
though one thing was too much.
Resting tea and biscuits,
upon a rabbit hutch.

Cheek

I have some running buddies,
who give me lots of cheek,
or am I the cheeky one,
and they are nice and meek?

Not all of them are runners,
some ride, swim or box.
I know a lady rower,
who likes to see a cox.

'You are incorrigible',
I know I have been called.
If my mother heard me,
I'm sure she'd be appalled.

Sometimes my mouth operates,
before my brain says 'Stop.'
Too late the words are said,
I wish the ground would drop.

I'm lucky that these people,
all have hearts of gold.
They tolerate my humour,
ignoring when I'm bold.

Despite my rude banter,
I can be kind within,
but my mouth ignores this,
and much I spout is sin.

The kindness that's inside me,
comes from in my wife.
Loving and supportive,
she is my happy life.

The banter contained within me,
has a naughty part.
Being silly and cheeky,
warms me in my heart.

Now if I've ever cheeked you,
I hope I won't offend.
Take it as a compliment,
that you are one good friend.

Old and Grumpy

I'm getting old and grumpy,
as people block my way.
Standing there quite dumbly,
'excuse me,' I will say.

First, they ignore me.
I ask if I can go.
My brain it gets impatient,
their movement is so slow.

I am not invisible,
yet they are blocking me.
I find myself annoyed,
that they refuse to see.

I am seen as difficult,
if ever I talk back.
The ones who were rude,
feel I may attack.

Rudeness hits a raw nerve,
it wears my patience thin.
People seem oblivious,
which I see as a sin.

If you're kind and thoughtful,
I will keep quite calm,
but if you are rude to me,
my pulse will show alarm.

I know that it's within me,
the way that I react.
I could be much kinder,
and show a little tact.

But sadly, I am grumpy,
and getting older too,
so please don't be rude to me,
or I may bark at you.

Modern Life

Looking back at growing up,
an innocent time for me.
Time outdoors, kicking a ball,
and maybe climb a tree.

Music on a tape cassette,
never was a drag.
Winding with a pencil,
when tape began to snag.

TV was so simple,
with channels, one to three.
Smiling at a Bagpuss yawn,
and Pugwash crew at sea.

Then as I got older,
video games appeared.
Funny space invaders,
that no one thought was weird.

On our first computer,
we had three games to play.
Loading each from the tape,
seemed to take all day.

In anticipation,
staring at these screens,
hours of blank waiting,
all through our teens.

All these things were new to us,
exciting and quite nice.
Little did we realise,
these games became a vice.

Along came the Internet,
or World Wide Web you know.
If you remember dial up,
you will know how slow.

But it was new and fancy,
we didn't mind the wait.
Will that picture ever load?
Kept us up too late.

Is it that we're British,
and seem to like to queue?
Waiting, waiting, waiting,
page load overdue.

Now that things are quicker,
everyone expects.
Streaming high res video,
paired with limitless texts.

Life has got so noisy,
gets upon my wick,
all those passwords in my brain,
'Forgot,' I always click.

Someone's stolen my identity,
to take my cash from me.
All because that link, I clicked,
was bogus so you see.

People demand an upgrade,
then they break the screen.
Throwaway society,
makes me want to scream.

Now my digital assistant,
listens to my voice.
Browse through a playlist,
let it make a choice.

If you are far away,
we connect to you,
but if you're in the room with us,
ignore you we will do.

Do I find life complex?
Yes, of course I do.
Life is filled with overwhelm,
and quiet is overdue.

Now that I am older,
I choose a different game.
One where friends get to talk,
A full on silly reign.

Common Sense

Searching for some common sense,
but everywhere I go,
I'm finding lots of adults,
who seem a little slow.

These people, they aren't stupid,
and lots I'd say are smart,
yet stuff that is quite obvious,
gives their brains a fart.

Common sense is lacking,
in the world today.
I see my IT users,
and wish they'd go away.

I know that I am technical,
I see a different light,
but stuff that is so simple,
they fail to do it right.

People often rushing.
They know what to do.
Jumping in with both feet,
to find a pile of poo.

Common sense is trouble.
For if you have a lot,
you'll be left to fix things,
and do the sodding lot.

I find that I'm a cynic,
when clearing others mess.
Did they mean to do this,
and cause me great distress?

Either they are stupid,
and being rather dumb,
or they are bloody clever,
and offload every one.

Where are all the Thinkers?

Common sense is lacking,
in the world about.
Seems that lots of people,
all they do is shout.

Often social media,
tells them what to do.
There are many of followers,
lots without a clue.

Independent thought,
where have you gone?
Needing creativity,
to share with everyone.

Maybe some are scared,
in the media glare.
Don't know what they're doing,
ideas so threadbare.

Some can be so loud,
placed in their spotlight.
People listen dumbly,
speakers must be right.

Please don't follow blindly.
Make sound judgement calls.
If you follow an idiot,
don't be the one who falls.

Our children need to question,
to ask, 'What is true?'
Check their information,
what it means to you?

Fake news is all around us,
practice to deceive.
Where is all the trickery?
What can we believe?

I hope you'll take some comfort,
that some around are right.
Filter through the rubbish,
and let them shine a light.

And if you use your own voice,
in amongst the noise.
Please show your kindness,
with eloquence and poise.

Fearless

When you were really little,
how did you behave?
I'd say you were fearless,
throughout your growing wave.

You couldn't manage feeding,
and wore a nappy too,
but you were busy learning,
to do a potty poo.

When you first tried walking,
I'm sure you had a fall.
It didn't set you back,
or you'd not walk at all.

You didn't say words properly.
Maybe that's still true,
yet you have learned a language,
with words like pink and blue.

So you've become an adult.
Are you fearless now?
Will you just 'do it',
and figure out somehow?

If you answered - No.
What has held you back?
Is it fear of others,
that steers you off the track?

When you were a baby,
you really didn't care.
You put yourself first,
almost everywhere.

Now you are responsible,
with rules you must obey,
but do not let your fear,
block your path today.

Think of how you used to be,
learning all that stuff,
No challenge seemed too daunting.
You couldn't get enough.

And once you'd finished learning,
you gave yourself a rest.
Maybe being like baby,
could work out for the best.

Selfie Generation

In this new generation,
some seem so self-obsessed.
Taking fifty selfies,
to post the one that's best.

Got to update Instagram,
snapchat filters on.
Show me to the world.
Be seen by everyone.

Don't upload that photo.
Can't let friends see me.
Oh your post is horrid,
you've made me ugly.

A world of photo touching,
with lots of pics we take,
leads to misdirection,
if what we show is fake.

Out, come teasers and the trolls,
and cyber bully crowd.
Can we withstand it,
when they become too loud?

Fake news is all around us.
See what I just read.
When time comes for us to vote,
like sheep we may be led?

Some need to have their followers,
or they'll be in the cold.
As for me, I don't much care,
maybe as I'm old?

I admit my phone is active,
I scan it in the night.
Have I joined the selfie gen?
That doesn't sit quite right.

Looking to the future,
I fear a trend increase.
Crowded with this crap,
we need to have some peace.

Do I need some more likes?
I'm not sure it's a must.
Maybe just some good friends.
Ones that I can trust.

Family and Loved Ones

Big Irene

(Warning, this one is a little bit cheekier)

I'd like you to come with me.
There's someone you should meet.
She called Big Irene,
she's old and rather sweet.

If you have a problem,
she will tell you straight,
but if you need normal help,
you should probably wait.

She likes to have odd cars.
She's given them all names.
She loves to go topless,
driving down the lanes.

Irene is a dancer.
She loves a bit of tap,
and if you are nice to her,
you'll get a little clap.

Sometimes on the quiz team,
she gets a question right,
then she tells the world,
that she's the shining light.

She's travelled all the world,
and people they do say.
They can't forget the time,
when Irene came to play.

Now I should really clarify,
who Irene is to me.
I am her son in law,
and she is quite lovely.

** I sought permission from my mother in
law before including this one. She has been
known to drive with the top down but is
always fully clothed and respectable. She
also has cheeky humour and a big kind heart.

Grandchildren and Grandparents

Observations of generations,
some of which are true.
The oldest and the youngest,
affecting me and you.

Grandchildren and grandparents,
often have such fun.
Giggles and some naughtiness,
and then go back with mum.

Grandparents love their grandchildren,
though like to give them back,
if they catch a whiff,
of dirty nappy sack.

Should they give them sweeties,
before they head off home?
Watch them bounce off the walls,
as son or daughter groan.

Maybe pranking daddy,
would be a funny game.
All are feigning innocence.
We are not to blame.

Grandparents have worldly wisdom.
They know just how it feels.
Now to see their children squirm.
It kind of just appeals.

A Grandad and grandma,
or nanna if you please,
love their grand offspring,
and can be quite a tease.

Now some are like a parent,
in this busy world of ours.
Mum and dad are working,
what seems to be all hours.

Some children who are little,
they love the older folk,
though some can be quite scary.
It isn't any joke.

They see grandad snoring,
with his hairy nose,
slumped upon the sofa,
with odd and baggy clothes.

At teatime grandad burps,
and then lets rip a fart.
The youngest they just giggle,
keen to play a part.

I hope your family sharing,
brings you thoughts of gold.
All too quickly young will age,
and some may sadly fold.

Take these precious moments,
fill your lives with glee.
Smile and be silly,
and live life happily.

The Modern Mum

The 6 am alarm.
Eyes, I fix them tight.
I just went to sleep,
I'm sure it's still the night.

Alarm, it is repeating,
nagging all the while.
My brain it is turgid,
unwilling to compile.

The sound is so insistent.
I wish I could ignore.
I look across and feel,
despair at partner's snore.

I get up and I feel it,
icy cold on feet.
I did this all yesterday.
My life is on repeat.

I ask the kids to wake up.
All they do is moan.
Incredible just how slowly,
these zombies seem to roam.

'I've lost my homework,'
comes a plaintive voice.
'Where did you leave it?'
like they'll give me a choice.

We look high and low,
though cannot sort it out.
The children they are moaning,
they think it's all my fault.

At breakfast with the kids,
they just muck about.
I look on despairingly,
and in the end, I shout.

Half fed and quite angry,
we head off to the car.
Take the cherubs to the school,
amid a tug of war.

Sitting at some traffic lights,
they mention dress up day.
Underneath my breath,
I'm muttering, 'oh yay,'

We cobble up some outfits,
with seconds left to spare,
then drop them at the school,
though they don't seem to care.

My kids they are complaining,
as costumes that they see,
all seem so much better,
and so they're blaming me.

I leave them all at school,
and go to earn some cash,
though wish I'd had a cuppa,
before my morning dash.

Two hours later.
I get that special call.
My children, they are poorly,
I must collect them all.

I sigh and apologise,
though the boss is quite good.
One day he may sack me,
just where I am stood.

At home, the kids are better.
Why'd they send them home?
What was the school thinking,
when they picked up the phone?

Later in evening,
I cook a lovely meal,
Kids see all the veggies,
and gone is all appeal.

After I am washing up,
where most goes in the bin,
kids complain they're hungry.
I cannot seem to win.

Now I'm doing laundry,
and picking up their mess.
They are into gaming,
ignoring my distress.

Partner he is home at last.
Yay, that's help I see,
but he is tired and stressed,
and wants support from me.

I settle him in comfort,
and hear his tales of woe,
and wonder if there's interest,
in me that he will show?

No, he keeps on talking,
about some meeting crap,
like I've had it easy,
and all I did was nap.

I ask about a card,
'Soon your mums birthday.'
'Oh, I thought you'd sort it.
You know what to say.'

Finally I sit down,
to do an online shop.
Hardly relaxation,
and I just want to drop.

Bedtime for the kids,
but they refuse to go.
'Just another episode,
we just have to know.'

I look to my husband.
He says, 'Let them stay,'
Their schoolwork it will suffer,
but he just looks away.

Now I start to buckle.
The day it has been long.
All I feel is drained,
something here is wrong.

Eventually, the tv ends,
and after lots of huff,
the kids go to their beds,
though I have had enough.

Exasperated and tired,
I read by bedside light.
Why is it always me,
to tuck them in at night?

Incredibly, at long last,
he washes just one cup,
then stands there expecting,
both my thumbs are up.

He looks at me and says,
'You should get some rest,'
I'm too tired to argue,
so head off to my nest.

My head is on my pillow,
and all I want is sleep,
but mind is oh so active,
and I just want to weep.

At last, the sleep it comes,
but only for a blink,
woken by child,
asking for a drink.

And here I am.
It's 6 am again.
Snoring by my side.
I think I've gone insane.

My Eyes

See yourself through my eyes.
I see such warmth and light.
You have an inner sparkle,
that makes things feel alright.

Even when you're weary,
your golden heart remains.
All the time I spend with you,
is always filled with gains.

I know you look upon yourself,
with different view to me.
Often you feel worthless.
Not what I can see.

Judging ourselves harshly,
what does it achieve?
Can you see through my eyes?
Wish you could believe?

Together we are stronger.
I ask you take my view.
You are quite amazing,
I love my time with you.

Siblings

Siblings may show rivalry,
and sometimes shirking blame.
Trying to get one over,
the other in a game.

If one is much younger,
all sweet and innocent,
the older may just pray on them,
with roughness and intent.

The young one for their virtue,
will sneak a little win,
by blaming the elder,
when they commit the sin.

Will they ever love each other?
I really cannot say.
Each day they get older,
and some will stray away.

But some will form a bond,
that's lifelong and it's strong,
defending their sibling,
even when they're wrong.

Friends can come and go,
but siblings are your kin,
and if you've got a good one,
everything's a win.

Grab Yourself a Rock

Many years ago,
as I first started out.
I looked for companionship,
to share what life's about.

I picked a few pebbles,
but none were any catch,
so I went back to searching,
and hoped to find my match.

I thought I had found one.
Turns out I was wrong.
This was a hefty boulder,
and I was not that strong.

The boulder wanted carrying,
and soon it weighed me down.
It sucked away the happiness,
until I thought I'd drown.

I could not sustain it.
I had to walk away.
The boulder kept on taking,
and still it takes today.

This had left me broken.
I was an awful mess.
Boulder took some more,
with me in wilderness.

Slowly I repaired myself,
and set to look again,
with meeting some odd pebbles,
within the dating game.

Confidence was waning.
I thought that I was stuck.
Somehow, I kept on searching.
I had a stroke of luck.

At last I found my rock.
I knew her right away.
Inside she has such kindness.
Bright for every day.

Within a month of meeting her,
ring and finger met.
People thought that we were mad,
but me and her were set.

If like me, you've struggled.
You think you are no good.
Choose to keep on trying,
or stay just where you're stood.

A rock who is strong for you,
when you are strong for them,
is the answer to your prayers.
I'm luckiest of all men.

The Parent

I am a parent,
and though you may not see.
I love my children dearly.
They mean the world to me.

Some days I am silent,
with stuff I do not share.
I carry some life burdens,
whilst they are unaware.

If I should go hungry,
so they will get to eat,
I'll always put them first,
within a mere heartbeat.

My children may not notice,
I think of them this way,
but I will do my best for them.
Today and every day.

I do not have much money,
and some say I'm not smart,
yet I will listen, and I'll care,
with all my parent heart.

They can always come to me,
whatever life may throw.
I will love and comfort them,
absorbing their sorrow.

They can take a piece of me,
so they may surely thrive.
I'll be very happy,
to see them so alive.

They may not be my blood,
or even part of me,
but if I am their carer,
then that is what I'll be.

Now if I'm really truthful,
some days I will be sad.
They may really drain me,
or make me very mad.

The thing with those moments,
I'll rant and I could curse,
but when all is said and done,
I'll put thoughts in reverse.

I'll stow away my anger,
return to do what's right.
The unappreciated taxi,
that drives them through the night.

I hope one day they'll realise,
I gave a loving hand,
and they may become parents,
who'll come to understand.

The Friendship Bank Account

I was introduced today,
to a simple way to be.
I look after you,
and you look after me.

I am not saying a partnership,
where we have to wed.
I do not mean silliness,
ending in the bed.

This isn't giving to receive.
Do not take that track.
Though if you offer humour,
you'll get that cheek right back.

It doesn't involve money,
or paying all your bills.
It doesn't mean a big old car,
or other fancy frills.

It can be quite simple,
when your life hits a bump.
A good friend will be there,
to lift you from your slump

If you make a deposit,
with kindness shown one day.
A friend can take a withdrawal from you,
when their need comes your way.

Each side they offer.
We do not keep a count,
but as long as it is fairly even,
keep this bank account.

* This poem was originally published in
Dipping Toes in Literary Waters – Volume 2.

Self-Care, Care for others and when things aren't quite right

The Imposter

I am an imposter,
I am not like you.
Compare myself to peers,
and watch what you all do.

You make it look so easy.
I really wonder how.
My mind it flails wildly.
What do I do now?

I struggle with the basics,
whilst you all understand.
My mind it's in overdrive,
I need a helping hand.

Am I the only one,
who seems is all at sea?
Do others feel the same,
or is it only me?

Those who are successful,
and some who've made a mark.
I am stuck confused,
forever in the dark.

Yet others they are like me.
Just the do not admit.
They quietly admire me,
whilst feeling they're the twit.

None of us like judgement.
Sometimes we feel fake.
Yet here we all are trying,
so give yourself a break.

Imposter syndrome, is it?
Put it to one side.
Keep on moving forwards,
and see some growth inside.

Reflections

Reflections in the mirror,
looking back at me.
Old with lots of wrinkles,
is that what others see?

Where did all the years go?
How'd I get this way?
Looking in my mirror,
all I see is grey.

The mirror doesn't lie,
but if it tells the truth.
I must be aged sixty.
A long way from my youth.

My mind may lack its sharpness,
my memory could have gone,
but I am rather happy,
I repeat to everyone.

Maybe I am harsh,
as I look upon myself.
Despite my blurry eyes,
I am in reasonable health.

I run and do some kettlebells,
though these do make me ache.
My lovely wife she shrugs at me,
'You're old for goodness sake.'

Am I fairly happy,
with the things I do?
Do I have a legacy,
to pass from me to you?

I may be lacking wealth,
and could be wisdom too.
I hope you'll think quite fondly,
as I do think of you.

My mind may lack its sharpness,
my memory could have gone,
but I am rather happy,
I repeat to everyone.

The Flag

As I wave my flag of white,
I gaze into the evening night,
and wonder of the things I feel,
a mighty weight that is so real.

Maybe if I truly try,
to search within the starry sky,
to see somewhere if I can find,
kindly thoughts I must remind.

For if I find life's weight too much,
I may crumble or some such,
and if I fall what will they say,
if I broke and fell away?

When you see that people care,
take that love and don't despair.
Find your flag that was so white,
and paint anew in colours bright.

Wave your flag, high and wide,
build yourself with love inside,
and if you see a friend may sag,
help them paint a coloured flag.

The Heffalump

As I trod upon the scales,
a voice inside said eek.
Pressing both my feet right down,
the floor began to creek.

The number I expected,
wasn't on the dial.
Something higher than I would like,
didn't make me smile.

I went back to the bedroom,
and felt I had to swear.
The mirror showed a swollen tum,
how did that get there?

Looking at my profile,
which really wasn't flat.
I felt hugely ugly,
to be so awfully fat.

Shock and disbelief,
flooded through my brain.
What had really happened,
to cause a mighty gain?

Was it the ice cream,
or biscuits paired with cheese?
Was it my nodding head,
when pudding offered please?

I exercise I told myself,
I should be quite trim.
But then there's all the junk I eat,
as though I am a bin.

I thought back to parkrun,
and how I huffed and puffed.
Have a race this weekend,
think I may be stuffed.

Excuses swam about,
and then I went to say.
This must be due to someone else,
I must make them pay.

Slowly I accepted,
that I had scoffed the food.
Then guilt came in behind me,
to put me in sad mood.

I felt really awful,
that I had been so bad.
Then anger flooded through my brain,
made me feel quite mad.

It wasn't just me that I had hurt,
as I had bought some crap.
Shared with those around me,
I deserve a slap.

My hips and knees are aching,
and sometimes gums may bleed.
I know I scoff the sugar,
my body doesn't need.

So now I feel a heffalump,
heavy and rather blue.
Worth nothing to anyone,
a diet is overdue.

The weight it is quite naughty,
as slowly it grows some more.
I close my eyes and hide it,
until I can't ignore.

I always feel so tired,
at the end of every day.
So cooking fresh and healthy,
seems so far away.

Why do we do this?
I tried to work it out.
Cause I'm bloody stupid,
my mind did loudly shout.

I sat and quietly thought,
feeling quite a knob.
Did my wife still love me,
though I'm quite a blob?

From all these low feelings,
I changed to feel quite bright.
I drew a line in the sand,
to start to do things right.

Of course my wife loves me,
and I feel just the same.
Together we are wonderful,
despite our weighty gain.

I know that I have forgotten,
to watch all that I do eat.
I didn't count the biscuits,
or that naughty treat.

I also know that if I plan,
to eat some healthy food.
My sleep pattern will improve,
and so a happier mood.

Eating treats now and then,
really is ok.
As long as we only have a tiny bit,
and not every day.

So am I still a heffalump?
Maybe just for now.
But I am giving this attention,
to return to feeling wow.

I also want to pledge support,
to my darling wife.
As it means the world to me,
for her to be happy in life.

Inner Critic

I have an inner critic,
that often speaks to me.
Saying I am useless,
and not who I should be.

It mentions lots of things.
Times when I fell short.
Listing lots of stuff.
A sad, unkind report.

I find I can't ignore it,
though I'd like to try,
but it is always niggling.
I never quite know why.

It feeds my insecurities.
I think that I am weak,
that I am unworthy,
and really shouldn't speak.

Now if these observations,
had come from friend or foe.
I'd get a bit annoyed,
and tell them where to go.

Because the voice is mine,
I think it may be true.
Must be somehow valid.
There's stuff I didn't do.

I know that I am coping.
I might not be so weak,
and with this open mindset
there's balance I can seek.

My inner critic lives,
but when it's had its say.
I'll see a different narrative,
and choose this other way.

Sorry from an Anxious Friend

Do people hate me,
as I'm feeling sad?
Should I shut away,
contain a head that's bad?

Should I lie,
to hide away my mood?
Is it better,
sat alone to brood?

Inside I'm a kind person,
who struggles to break out.
My brain is such a turmoil,
inwardly I shout.

Over thought answers,
I could give to you,
or saying, 'I'm fine',
which isn't really true.

I'm trying to protect you,
my friends and family.
So you don't see,
my brains calamity.

I feel really stupid,
simple things a test.
If I can't cope,
then hiding is the best.

I'm scared, there I said it,
of what you'll think of me.
But now that I have said it,
support I can see.

I'll find other kind folks,
and open up to them.
Seek out empathy,
it's such a hidden gem.

The sad voice within my head,
withdraws me even more.
Bring in others,
who let you see the score.

I'm not alone, others know,
what I'm going through.
Those that love me,
and want me happy too.

So sorry that I hid away,
when things became so bad.
I listened to my inner voice,
which caused me to feel sad.

I know ahead I'll wobble,
but will have you by my side,
and I will choose openness,
rather than to hide.

Isolation

Trials in isolation,
a headspace sat in me.
My head is a closed off box,
that no one else can see.

I'm lucky and I'm happy,
though have some struggles too.
Life is how I want it,
filled with all of you.

But how do I manage things,
overwhelm is often on?
Stuff that keeps me wide awake,
till the night is almost gone.

Control what I can,
and put that phone away.
All those Facebook messages,
can wait another day.

There will be stress around us,
that you can't change at all.
How you all react to it,
will show you stand or fall.

If you stand and cope with things,
that really is quite good,
but if you fall, then get back up,
to where you had been stood.

I know that seems simplistic,
and doesn't always gel,
but choosing strong and happy,
is better than some hell.

Before you get to bedtime,
empty your mind, if you can.
Read a book quite quietly,
for sleep to be the plan.

If you have a load of jobs,
rattling in your head,
put them in a notebook,
before you turn for bed.

I know it isn't easy,
and I don't get it right,
though being dark and cosy,
can help you in the night.

Now if your lovely partner,
snores a bit too loud,
don't cover her head with a pillow,
to drown the nasal sound.

For if you really love them,
as I know you do.
Remember this awesome person,
who wants to be with you.

The Onion

I think that I'm an onion,
yes you read that right.
I know I'm not brown,
or sour if you bite.

I love to help my friends.
That's always been ok,
though every time I offer help,
a layer peels away.

Now I'm feeling tired,
and worn to my core.
I need layers returning,
to be a whole once more.

A few they've been fabulous,
though some have been a drain.
Sad when friends don't back you,
and things begin to wane.

Now my circles narrowed,
though I'll still back a friend.
Others drop from prominence,
if everything's pretend.

Slowly if I'm careful,
my layers will grow back,
and if I choose friends wisely,
then I'll get back on track.

Ready to Explode

I'm ready to explode,
at some idiots that I see.
Making things more difficult,
for all including me.

Always crisis management,
which we don't really need.
Nothing I can do,
just suck it up indeed.

Progress it is painful,
strategy unknown.
What the hell is happening?
No team but all alone.

The thing that makes me saddest,
is I really care,
but being blocked from action,
drives me to despair.

I'm angry and frustrated,
we've had time through the year.
Those days are now all wasted,
and look the deadlines here.

Nothing ever happens.
Around we go again.
All could be much better,
it really is a shame.

Hired for my skills,
to help the company through,
then blocked from any action,
as though I'm stuck in glue.

I can't step outside my silo.
Discouraged from talking too.
All of this is frowned upon,
No sharing with me and you.

I'd love to be a team player,
where everyone's involved.
Ideas and innovation,
all are teamwork gold.

Until that day it happens,
which I doubt it will.
I will do as I'm asked,
but watch it go downhill.

Running Mojo

I've lost my running mojo.
Where can it be?
It wasn't there yesterday,
as I ate too much tea.

I looked behind the sofa,
I couldn't see it there.
It wasn't in my drawers,
as they held underwear.

I've been a massive piggy.
I've scoffed too much food.
Now I feel a fatty,
which puts me in a mood.

My breathing's gotten heavy,
as I lug all my weight.
I know that I am guilty,
with food piled on my plate.

Injury and niggles,
have added to my woe.
This with all the pounds,
made my mojo go.

I'll say to all you people,
that I will do a run.
I'll have to shake a leg,
and really shift my bum.

And if you see my mojo,
send it back to me.
So I can run more races,
and breathe quite healthily.

Silence

Silence is golden,
or so they often say,
but silence can be sadness,
when viewed another way.

When you see me quiet.
How am I, you think?
Am I being moody,
or am I in the pink?

When in a church or library,
quiet is the rule,
but hush when we're together,
doesn't seem so cool.

If you feel unsure,
when someone close won't speak.
Don't mirror their silence.
Don't be one who's weak.

It may be they won't talk,
and that could be ok,
but being there for them,
can really make their day.

And if you are the one,
who shuts all others out.
Don't isolate completely,
those that stick about.

We all have our burdens,
which may weigh us down.
Allow those who value us,
to undo every frown.

I Must Always do it

I must always do it,
with no help from you.
I have to stand upon my feet,
to be both real and true.

Accepting any help?
That's not the path for me.
I will do my thing,
in quiet dignity.

And if I let you help me,
then gone is my self-worth.
I cannot be beholden,
to others on the earth.

As I make my progress,
if it's only small,
I'll keep myself all quiet,
until I'm feeling tall.

Now this does a disservice,
to those who've been your friend.
By choosing to ignore them,
likely you'd offend.

Friends, they won't judge you,
if your friends are true,
but if you ignore them,
then they may pass on through.

Now you are reading this,
and saying, 'this is me.'
Contact those who care for you,
and thank them graciously.

Take me to the Edge

Take me to the edge.
Let's see what lays beyond.
Will it be too scary,
or stuff of which I'm fond?

The thing with staying safe,
and only in one spot,
life's so very short.
There may be just one shot.

I do not mean be reckless,
and please don't be unkind.
Seek out new experiences.
Improve your state of mind.

Take that first step forward,
towards a goal unknown.
Push your boundaries back,
with friends or on your own.

You will find the edge,
is always moving back,
but as you move towards it,
I hope you'll get the knack.

By visiting new places,
or learning something new,
you'll learn some life riches.
Look back and see you grew.

Who am I?

Am I sweet and succulent,
or rotten to the core?
Am I rather interesting,
or am I quite a bore?

Do I offer kindness,
or will I show distrust?
Am I very sensitive,
or am I prone to lust?

Can I be impatient,
or do I give my time?
Shall I go tee total,
or have a glass of wine.

Am I always tired,
or full of energy?
Am I really lazy,
or do I find a way?

Am I very generous,
or am I rather tight?
Do I like the morning,
or am I up at night?

In truth I am all of these,
and which one I will be,
depends how you treat me.
So try and you will see.

Don't Apologise

No need to say you're sorry,
if your laughter is too loud,
or if you've too much make up,
and stand out from a crowd.

Do not say you're sorry,
if your outfit is quite brash,
or if you wear your hair,
with ribbons and a sash.

How you dress and who you are,
are things we want to see.
Always try to be yourself,
and do it fearlessly.

Love your awkward weirdness,
the sarcasm and the fun.
Live your life, be yourself,
and welcome everyone.

Your time on earth is limited.
Do not be apart.
Give your life some meaning,
and love with all your heart.

How am I Really?

How am I really?
Do you ever ask?
Are you seeing smiles?
Is it just my mask?

What if I'm not coping?
My head is screaming out.
'Why can't you see I'm broken?'
Of that there is no doubt.

I feel a wall of silence,
believe that you don't care.
I think the world is better,
if I'm no longer there.

I know that some do love me,
and I love them too,
but also, I feel worthless,
no good to me or you.

Some stuff I am hearing,
bad and so unkind.
I've no capacity left in me.
No way I can unwind.

I'm tired now, it's draining.
Perhaps my time is nigh?
I've grown so very weary,
gone is all the high.

Maybe if I died,
the pain would finally end,
then suddenly everyone,
would want to be my friend.

So if you get to see me,
before it is too late.
When I say I'm 'Fine.'
Stop and think and wait.

I may not feel like talking,
I may not want a hug,
but knowing you are offering,
may stop me pull the plug.

Just One Word

Sometimes I write one word.
Yes just the one.
Put it on the page,
and then I may be done.

This tiny amount,
of no consequence,
yet each word added,
builds significance.

The word that I wrote,
some days it could be wrong.
It doesn't seem to fit,
I'm sure it won't belong.

Tomorrow I may edit,
and change it if I need.
Adding some more words,
despite my ponderous speed.

My project before me,
stretches my poor brain.
Self-doubt and overwhelm,
each will stake a claim.

The thing with big projects,
as you move on through.
Gradually you see,
what you can really do.

I may lack some style.
My grammar may be poor.
One or two characters,
perhaps should see the door.

To me that's learning.
To me that is ok.
I can take on board,
critiques that people say.

Some days I will add,
more than just one word.
My writing it will grow,
and readers may applaud.

To get to this place,
I just need to try.
Add another word,
and watch them multiply.

The Monster

I have this little monster,
that lays beneath my bed.
When I ask for peace and quiet,
it shouts at me instead.

I close my eyes and hope for rest,
which never seems to come.
The monster talking underneath,
really makes me glum.

I pull a pillow across my face,
can I block it out?
Sadly no, I still can hear,
that awful monsters shout.

Another hour passing,
sleep won't come my way.
Naughty monster chattering,
through to break of day.

Tired and harassed,
I reach another night,
thinking of the monster,
what makes it sound so right?

In this game, what is your name?
Why do you taunt me so?
I feel cracked, you'll get me sacked,
you have to let me go.

Monster - who are you,
to keep me wide awake?
My brain is feeling muddled,
shut up for goodness sake.

The monster it is quieter now,
as though it's quite appalled.
Search your head for things you dread,
you know what I am called.

Self-doubt and anxiety,
are names I'm sure you know.
You my friend, lack belief,
uncertain how to grow.

This came as a surprise to me,
but made me smile, it's true.
Believe and value in yourself,
and others will do to.

Now I've tamed my monster,
I rarely feel quite sad,
monster shouts when I achieve,
and makes me feel quite glad.

If you have a monster,
love yourself a bit,
the kindness that you show yourself,
will make a happier fit.

What we Choose to do

With two hands we are given,
we could choose to clap,
or offer up a shoulder rub
instead some opt to slap.

Arms we have for hugging,
and sharing warmth and love.
Some they will push away,
avoiding all things snug.

Feet we have for walking,
or running if we choose,
or feet could be for kicking,
when they are to abuse.

We have two ears for music,
for learning or a song.
Pompous prefer their own voice,
even when they're wrong.

We have two eyes for seeing,
to take in all life's joy,
else focus in on all that's bad,
and likely to annoy.

A mouth we have for talking,
and offering lots of praise,
or shouting anger and abuse,
with voice prone to raise.

A heart we have for kindness,
and love we give and share,
or turn it black as coal,
and do not choose to care.

So, if you have these things.
I know that not all do.
Choose the kinder path,
reflect it back to you.

The Cup

The cup that I pour from,
it seems it has run dry.
Emotional bombardments,
that make me want to cry.

One after another,
struggles came my way.
Wondering what I should do?
Will I cope today?

I said my cup was empty,
and yet this can't be true.
Here I am with writing,
drawing strength anew.

So maybe I am frazzled,
with patience running thin.
I know I'm not completely right,
but somehow, I will win.

I will back my friends,
though please just bear with me.
Right now, my cup has little in,
So, treat me gently.

Batteries

Battery needs charging,
lights are feeling dim.
Looking deep inside me,
for energy from within.

It all seems so absent.
I always seem so tired.
When my bedtime comes,
suddenly I'm wired.

If it was an afternoon,
on a sunny day.
I'd barely close my eyes,
and soon be on my way.

What is it about night-time,
that keeps us wide awake?
Worrying about silly stuff?
A waste for goodness sake.

Sometimes on a rest day,
I feel the energy sap.
Oddly if I'm active,
no need to take that nap.

When I eat some rubbish,
surprise, it makes me fat,
makes my sleep a struggle,
oh well fancy that.

Tackling all the stresses,
shake that overwhelm.
Steer toward a straighter path,
with you upon the helm.

The more you can fix things,
or face a problem true,
the easier your sleep will come.
A sweet dream earned for you.

Me, Just me

I'm feeling rather flawed,
but that's ok with me.
Embracing all my quirks,
to live quite happily.

I don't want to be perfect,
an aim I cannot reach.
Content with forward motion,
to learn and maybe teach.

My teeth they could be straighter,
and more hair on my head,
but I don't need those things.
I'll stay this way instead.

I'm learning how behaviour,
and actions that I take,
influence the outcome,
a good life I can make.

I used to make bad choices,
that left me feeling sad.
Depressed and anxious,
a mood filled with bad.

Now I am much stronger,
though wobble now and then,
but exercise and friendship,
brings me back again.

I am so very lucky,
to see a world in light.
My mind alert to possibilities,
to make a future bright.

I know others struggle,
sometimes I can help,
but even if I can't,
message me and yelp.

For those who have wronged me,
it used to cause me pain.
Dwelling upon these things,
dragged me down again.

Now I've made some changes.
The past has been and gone.
I have chosen happier,
supporting everyone.

I'll never be the quickest,
and diet could improve,
but I will guarantee,
I'll shake my bum and move.

The Sugar Pig

The shout of the sugar pig,
near the sweetie aisle.
Squealing in my ear so loud,
it's really rather vile.

I walk past all the sweeties,
louder gets the squeal.
'Get that bar of chocolate.
I've barely had a meal.'

I relent and buy the chocolate,
and soon it has gone.
Squealing in my head again.
'Let's have another one.'

'Shhhh,' I tell my brain,
I know it is a trick.
If I keep on eating,
it will make me sick.

My willpower it is rubbish,
and the pig it won't be quiet.
Soon I'm shovelling sugar again,
despite the awful diet.

Now I cannot sleep again,
and yes, I do know why.
The squeal in my head won,
it makes me want to cry.

If it was a toddler tantrum,
I'm sure I would stand strong.
Despite the child's ranting,
I'd firmly say 'You're wrong.'

But when it comes to sugar binging,
I often can't say 'No.'
Even though I feel so bad,
and energy is so low.

It may be like quitting smoking,
which is a thing I've done.
Have a pause in the shop,
take a breath and then move on.

I know that if I keep up,
with each mindful choice,
I will be much healthier,
the pig will lose its voice.

So every time you hear it,
know the squeal's a lie.
Move past the sweetie aisle,
let the junk go by.

I'm not saying rid everything,
that is sweet and nice,
but balance and eat mindfully,
to control your sugar vice.

The Wobble Tum

I looked down this morning,
just as I awoke.
I saw a wobbly tummy,
that wasn't any joke.

When last, I really checked,
I'm sure it wasn't there,
but looking down today,
spread is everywhere.

I remember many years ago,
when I was rather young.
Laying in the sun,
(boxers not a thong).

Yes, I know that image,
will make you all go yuck.
Now I am quite different,
with fat that I can tuck.

When I was much younger,
I did more exercise.
Always on a bike,
showing lovely thighs.

I kept myself quite active.
Meals were cooked at home.
Didn't drink too much,
which kept me in some tone.

One day without notice,
the spreading, it began.
Don't know what had happened,
but now I'm twice the man.

Of course I'm not that lazy,
though I am often tired.
When it's close to teatime,
I feel that I've expired.

With energy depleted,
and jobs I have to do.
Quick and naughty food,
which makes me feel like poo.

So now that I have noticed,
my tummy and its wobble.
Should I reverse this,
decrease the intake gobble?

It isn't very easy.
I'd really like to try.
Things in moderation,
except for apple pie.

Maybe in the future,
the wobble, it could go,
though even with my wobble,
I'm the me that you all know.

Dominos

Dominos lined up,
all are tall and proud.
Look inside my mind,
seems I'm safe and sound.

Each domino within me,
is a part of life.
One may be a daughter,
one may be my wife.

Many of them are my friends,
could be good or bad.
Some bring happiness,
others make me sad.

We all need these dominos.
Try to stand them tall.
Careful we don't knock them,
as they are sure to fall.

If one gets knocked over,
through argument or a frown.
Pick that domino back up,
else others could drop down.

If one knocks to another,
pray that you are quick.
If they all collapse,
then you will feel quite sick.

But if the worst it happens,
and all of them just fell.
Friends can help you start again,
on a path to being well.

The Jigsaw

If life could be a picture,
with pieces that we choose.
Stick together good bits,
and you may never lose.

Now if you hate your picture,
clear it all away.
Find some other pieces,
starting straight away.

Sadly in our lives,
are things we can't control.
Like passing of a loved one,
leaving quite a hole.

But when sad times they find us,
don't throw that piece away.
Keep that loving picture,
like they are here today.

Your jigsaw may be missing,
something you deserve.
Incomplete, frustrating,
really hits a nerve.

When your puzzle picture,
doesn't seem to work.
Pick up different pieces,
to create some new artwork.

If your jigsaws complex,
of pieces there are lots.
Life may be haphazard,
you cannot join the dots.

Make your jigsaw simple,
pieces make them few.
Soon you'll have your picture,
good life embracing you.

The Well Runs Dry

What do we do,
if our well, it runs dry?
Do we sit and wait,
till rain falls from the sky?

And whose job is it,
to fill the well again?
Is it always down to me,
or will you take the strain?

When those who are beside us,
create a barren void.
Do we let it happen,
and then we feel annoyed?

Then comes awkward silence,
when once there was a pact.
The distant friend must action,
to keep support intact.

And if they do not bother,
the well it dries for good.
Sadly only dust remains,
where friendship once was stood.

There is a need for balance.
I will fill your cup,
but don't take me for granted,
or I'll seal the well back up.

Radiators and Drains

Some people they can radiate,
some people they can drain,
Some days I find I switch between,
which really is a pain.

It may be I am tired,
or maybe I am bored.
It may be you have pushed my button,
which I have not ignored.

I could be feeling guilty,
for crap that I just ate,
or maybe I'm impatient,
and will not want to wait.

For some of us we meet in life,
their glass is barely full.
They have views they often hold,
though some may seem quite dull.

A drain can have their reasons,
and some find life quite tough.
Whatever they are feeling,
we really shouldn't scoff.

Please don't judge those who drain,
whether quiet or lacking cheer.
Who knows what thoughts are lurking,
under a veneer.

Others that we find in life,
are filled to overflow.
Streaming positivity,
it seems they surely know.

Even those we sometimes meet,
are cheery day and night.
They may have life problems,
hanging out of sight.

There are so many different people,
in the world with you,
and though they fill the room, with light or
gloom,
they offer good things too.

A pessimist offers caution,
when fools could rush right in.
On optimist takes things bad,
and gives a brighter spin.

Whatever type of person,
you may be today.
Walk some steps, now and then,
in others shoes I say.

You may find some insight,
that you thought you had lost.
All for a little mindfulness,
hopefully at minor cost.

I am not a mindset coach,
who knows about these things.
I just observe and commentate,
to see if goodness brings.

Now I know that some people,
will always be quite glum,
and no amount of sparkle,
will fill them full of fun.

I do not have an answer,
for all so low in mood.
Some folks choose to spend their life,
in meek and sombre brood.

Whether we choose to radiate,
or if we choose to drain,
figuring out what life is about,
can bring you back again.

And as for me, you'll surely see,
I can feel quite blue.
I hope you'll treat me kindly,
as I will treat you too.

Worry

Why do I worry,
what people think of me?
Lots of tired thoughts,
all uncertainty.

Fretting and stress,
beliefs that could be true.
Unsure in my mind,
of what I mean to you.

I know some people like me,
but what if I fall short?
Does it affect me,
what I think you thought?

Of course it shouldn't,
I should live for me,
but you are all in my world,
affecting what I see.

It's not those who hate me,
that cause me to feel low.
I don't give you any time,
you can't stop me grow.

It's all you lovely folks,
of whom I care a lot,
that cause me all to worry
turns my brain to rot.

So what can I do,
to ditch the worry head?
Accept that I am awesome,
and be myself instead.

Whatever choices I can make,
some people will be proud.
Even if I fail,
support it can be found.

So will I stop my worries?
Not sure I ever could,
but knowing you're beside me,
makes me feel so good.

Exercise

An exercise poem,
is one that's hard to write,
finding rhymes for burpees,
that do not sound all shite.

Some of us are cyclists
and some, they like to plank.
Searching out a rhyme for this,
I need a data bank.

Some of us are swimmers,
up and down the pool,
or if you are quite crazy,
in the sea so cool.

We may know some runners,
who may run just a mile,
whilst others manage ultras.
You all do make me smile.

If you are a beginner,
who cannot run a K.
Keep on pushing forwards.
You will another day.

Maybe you like football,
and kicking in the park,
or could it be the bootcamp,
that lights your precious spark.

Some may do Pilates,
or yoga in the heat.
Some of you look forward,
to your sweaty treat.

It may be you like lifting,
and muscles that can grow,
or are you a boxer,
with punches you do throw?

Whether you can snowboard,
or maybe you're a skier.
Perhaps you're the canoeist,
riding down the weir.

Up a mountain some may go,
it really is so high.
Amazing so much energy,
you feel that you could fly.

You of course can pick and choose,
how to spend your day.
Be a couch potato,
if that will be your way.

I am sure that you do know,
the consequence of that.
Munch the pies, see your thighs,
may grow a bit too fat.

Keeping body healthy,
really is the start.
A healthy brain, that you maintain,
with friendships of the heart.

There are people out there,
who exercise like you.
My advice, if they are nice,
stick to them like glue.

I Want To

I want to, I want to,
I want to raise my hand,
to ask you that question.
I hope you'll understand.

I'm nervous, I'm nervous.
What will you think of me?
Suddenly I feel foolish,
red cheeks that you will see.

Oh no! Oh no!
I think the chance has gone.
Why didn't I say something?
Am I all that dumb?

I'm angry, so angry,
with brain in retreat.
Why was I silent,
pinned within my seat?

It's safe, it's safe,
that's the reason why.
Does safe mean nothing,
just life is passing by?

I wonder, I wonder,
if I opened up?
Could I ask that question,
without choking up.

Maybe, just maybe,
I will end up hurt,
and staying so silent,
will save me from the dirt.

What if, what if,
I speak my question loud?
Will I be ignored,
and lost within the crowd?

It's done, it's done,
I've voiced my message out,
I didn't waver,
or ever feel in doubt.

The people, those people,
they've stopped to hear me say.
They haven't become angry,
or sent me on my way.

They're smiling, they're happy,
glad I'm joining in.
I was so silly,
such slowness to begin.

I want to, I want to,
OK then yes I will.

Gin

When I've had a tough day,
and cannot seem to win,
I want my special potion.
(Basically it's gin).

Now booze in moderation,
may not be too bad,
but using it for stress relief,
is naughty just a tad.

You may have your chocolate,
or maybe it's ice cream.
There are alternative potions,
for when you need to scream.

And whilst gin's no solution,
though technically it is.
It means I do not strangle,
the ones who caused a tiz.

So if you need a potion,
raise a glass with me.
Together we will cope,
with the misery.

If we are quite careful,
one day we may find.
No need for gin for stress relief,
when people are unkind.

I Can't Run

I can't run, I'm just too slow,
Look at the others, watch them go.

I can't run, I'm overweight,
It won't ever happen, it's the cakes I ate.

I can't run, it's barely a hobble,
An extended tummy causes a wobble.

I can't run, I'm all the wrong shape,
Look at me, you'd think I'm an ape.

I can't run, it's much too dark,
Mustn't head out if I can't see the park.

I can't run, I mightn't do well,
Plus there's fear, what if I fell?

I can't run, it's way too tough,
When I get moving, I feel so rough.

I can't run, I'm scared you see,
If I go out, they'll laugh at me.

I can't run, it seems way too far,
So much easier to jump in a car.

I can't run, my brain says 'No',
My legs won't move, they refuse to go.

I can't run, I'm much too old,
Plus look outside, it seems so cold.

I can't run, my face gets red,
My breathing is laboured, I feel half dead.

I can't run, I've had a month off,
Just the thought is making me cough.

I can't run, I'm always tired,
If I get going, will feel I've expired.

I can't run, work is so busy,
Eventually home, making me dizzy.

I can't run, I've too much to do,
No time for me, just the kids and you.

I can't run, I feel so weak,
Another kilometre feels so bleak.

I can't run, my muscles say ouch,
Can't I return to that nice soft couch?

I can't run, I'm just no good,
Why do I bother, I'm just like dead wood?

I can't run, my tummy's all upset,
Must take Imodium to target the threat.

I can't run, I'll never get quicker,
Each attempt keeps making me sicker.

I can't run, there's a big hill,
Just the sight removes all of the thrill.

I can't run, they're all so fast,
If I run now, I might come last.

I can't run it's interval night,
Even saying it fills me with fright.

I can't run, fartlek you say?
Netflix and chill seems more my way.

I can't run, I just shouldn't go,
Look at my pace, I'm way too slow.

I can't run, my head feels so bad,
I just can't do it, makes me feel sad.

I can't run, I'll drag you all down,
Look at me, the worst in town.

I can't run, you're all so great,
Look at me, the person I hate.

I can't run, I'd probably fail,
I'm not a runner, merely a snail.

I can't run a marathon race,
Take three steps and fall on my face.

I can't run, I'm just a joker,
You're all awesome, I'm mediocre.

I can't write, oh wait, I did.

I Have a Little Nerve

I have a little nerve,
that's feeling slightly sore.
Someone has been rubbing it,
and now it's rather raw.

Interference and awkwardness,
is reaching me today.
Leaving me disheartened,
that they can be this way.

I'm trying to be reasonable,
I'm trying to be kind,
but this is never mirrored,
which puts me in a bind.

One day if I'm lucky,
all will get to see,
who caused the unpleasantness,
and find it wasn't me.

This isn't very nice,
and some may feel unfair,
but I'll keep on smiling,
and leave the crap elsewhere.

Now if you find that someone,
is getting on your nerves.
Don't get yourself all angry.
It's not what you deserve.

It may not be easy,
but you don't have to shout.
One day they will see some karma,
and all will level out.

Tumble

I think I took a tumble,
my brain is in retreat.
Tummy's gotten fat,
I'm staring at my feet.

Suddenly I'm lonely,
in a friendly crowd.
Want to hide away,
no good to be around.

I'm smiling and chatting,
but gone is inner glow.
Putting on a fake smile,
as mind is feeling low.

I'm quiet and not feeling it,
safer on my own.
Best I avoid your contact,
instead to be alone.

I know I'm being silly,
and people really care,
yet 3am I'm writing this,
sat in underwear.

Picking up some injuries,
and some who caused upset,
sent me on a nosedive,
which hasn't upturned yet.

Then some friends were staying,
we really hit the snacks.
Suddenly I'm fat again,
which stopped me in my tracks.

My running mojo's dwindled.
My sense of worth is fried.
Uncertain how best to behave,
so thinking I should hide.

Slowly I will come back out,
but if you see my face.
Accept I may be quiet,
in my anxious place.

I know that I am lucky,
though I'm tired too.
Just be patient with me,
as I battle with the blue.

A Few Personality Types

The Narcissist

'You said it' I said,
with lots of certainty.
'I didn't' you say,
'your fault never me.'

Others they listen,
agree that I was right.
Makes no jot of difference,
I'm blamed for all despite.

Anxiety, it creeps.
Is it always me?
You say I'm at fault.
It's all that you can see.

Control and greed.
Eroding me inside.
You say you're never wrong,
and then you just deride.

My eyes are clouded,
losing all self-worth.
You make out I am useless,
and grind me to the earth.

One day it happened,
you pushed me much too far.
Space within my head,
to see just what you are.

Slowly, I'm feeling,
anxiety it is less.
People can approach,
and they don't cause distress.

I'm happier, I've learned,
to trust that I'm ok,
and those that belittled,
well they can fall away.

You may keep choosing,
to blame and distort.
I'll take the path,
kindness and support.

The Optimist

I'm the eternal optimist,
nothing phases me.
Expecting the best outcome,
an ending happily.

Our team it may be losing.
The match is almost done.
I'll expect a miracle,
a game that can be won.

Take me to the races,
and back a horse or two.
Even with three legs,
our rider will come through.

Sitting an exam,
of course I'll get the grade.
I know I didn't study,
but I have got this made.

If all your health is failing,
and you're a sickly sight.
I'll expect recovery,
before we get to the night.

Some will say I'm foolish.
They just don't agree.
Life just isn't like that.
There's hardship there to see.

But I will just ignore them,
and keep my happy smile.
I'm the eternal optimist,
a winner all the while.

The Pessimist

A little ray of sunshine,
brightness for today.
When will the clouds come by,
to hide the sun away?

This is how things happen.
This is how I am.
One minute I'm okay,
but soon will be a jam.

I find that I am waiting,
full of ifs and buts.
Somethings heading my way,
to kick me in the guts.

My half full cup is leaking,
toast falls jammy side.
Where has all my luck gone?
Best I run and hide.

If I err on side of caution,
things won't disappoint.
You may think I'm negative,
but I think what's the point.

I may expect the worst,
but that's ok with me.
It may come as a surprise,
but I live happily.

I don't overreach,
and I don't expect too much.
I like how things are,
all within my touch.

Others that are just nice

Autumn

The sun sits low across the ground,
A small girl stoops to brush a mound,
Her tiny hand grasps a leaf of gold,
Despite the damp she feels quite bold.

A happy smile, an innocent face,
she waves her trophy about the space.
The golden flag that she has found,
shaken aloft with barely a sound.

Oh wow, cries mum, what have we here?
Sensing a moment filled with cheer.
Keep it safe and you'll be glad,
as losing your treasure may make you sad.

But mummy look there's hundreds more,
Scattered around across the floor.
Maybe we can kick them all,
so let's pretend and make a ball.

They laugh and dance and kick aloft,
lucky the leaves are nice and soft.
They fly everywhere, all around,
then settle again, across the ground.

Daughter dear, why do you feel,
that leaves should fall and form a seal?
Each year along the ground they lay,
waiting for a springtime day.

The girl paused in quiet thought,
then speaking quietly, she did report.
Mummy, do they die away,
to come again another day?

Yes, that's right you clever child,
after winter when things are mild.
The flowers bloom and new leaves form,
all around as things grow warm.

But that is then and here is now,
Enjoy your world so full of wow.
Autumn is a most beautiful time,
wonderful colours with golden shine.

Every day is a gift you see,
My time with you and yours with me,
Take the beauty and the fun,
Enjoy your day in the Autumn sun.

The Woods

As I walked within the woods,
I saw a great oak tree.
Walking past, I heard a gasp.
and a voice called after me.

"Do you like the woods my friend?
It's nice to see you here."
I spun around, to seek the sound,
But none were standing near.

Looking up and down,
I really scratched my head.
Spinning back around again,
a louder voice it said.

"Can you not see me?
It really is no joke.
I'm the tree before you,
the tall and mighty oak."

I looked a little closer.
Is someone pranking me?
Come on show yourself!
It cannot be a tree.

Feeling a little silly,
with no one else to see,
"ok then oak, it's not a joke,
why don't you talk to me?"

"You seemed so very happy,
to walk this way today.
I thought I'd say hi, as you walked by,
and see you on your way."

I spluttered as I heard these words,
looking for the source.
My brain would not accept,
a talking tree, of course.

Excitement flowed within me,
despite my spinning head.
Looking at the branches,
to hear the words it said.

Feeling slightly braver,
I thought I'd stay and talk.
Hoping that no ramblers,
would hear me whilst they walk.

I walked a little closer,
and quietly asked the tree.
"What advice can you share,
with someone just like me?"

"Always keep on growing,
as you reach towards the sky.
Stand tall and proud, within your crowd,
respecting you and I."

Now I listened eagerly,
and asked to hear some more.
Suddenly I'm interested,
this tree is not a bore.

"Remember your roots, eat green shoots,
and try to not be late.
Go out on a limb, learn to swim,
and of course hydrate."

"Get rid of all your dead wood,
and for goodness sake,
keep yourself well grounded,
so you bend before you break."

"Adapt to change,
and enjoy the view.
Always be confident,
in all that you do."

I could have listened all the night,
the tree, it spoke me.
But sadly darkness came along,
so off I went for tea.

I didn't hear the oak tree,
when next I walked that way.
But know the words it spoke to me,
are wise for every day.

If you go out to the woods,
but cannot hear a voice.
Love all that is around you.
It seems the obvious choice.

* This poem was originally published in
Dipping Toes in Literary Waters – Volume 2.

A Down Syndrome Poem

I'm told I have Down Syndrome.
Not sure what it means.
Mum says I am awesome,
the stuff of happy dreams.

I look a little different,
but that's ok with me,
as long as you are kind,
then I am quite happy.

Sometimes when I learn,
I want to take things slow.
Don't let that overshadow,
my kindly inner glow.

I love life experiences,
and things that I am shown.
I'll go at my speed,
and get there on my own.

I hope you won't avoid me,
for that would be a shame.
I am every bit your equal,
and Downs is just a name.

Take me as your friend,
and I'll be friends with you.
I'll share my smile and more,
as I am worth lots too.

The Autism Poem

A friend of mine's autistic.
'What is that you say?
Is he really mad,
or odd in every way?'

I cringe when I hear this,
for it is quite untrue.
My autistic friend,
is just like me or you.

She can sing a song,
or write a fiction book.
She'll run marathons,
and she may like to cook.

Her brain that's wired differently,
shouldn't cause alarm.
She's kind and intelligent,
with no intent of harm.

She may dislike loud noises,
or smells and blazing light.
Imagine how you would feel,
if things were always bright?

Sometimes this intensity,
becomes a bit too much.
She may shy away,
reluctant for your touch.

She has such a focus,
with sharp intellect.
Such a worthwhile lady,
who we should give respect.

I can't appreciate fully,
what autism's really like,
but I will treat with dignity,
as we may be alike.

The Sun it Shone

The flowers bloomed,
and sun it shone.
They didn't know,
what had gone on.

The sea it crashed,
upon the beach,
oblivious to,
the virus reach.

The day it went,
and then came night,
unaware of,
all our fright.

The world it turned,
just as before,
and then the people,
shut the door.

This simple act,
to hide away,
helped slow the spread,
and keep at bay.

The natural things,
they'll still be there,
so please hang on.
Do not despair.

The more we do,
to keep contained,
as scientists everywhere,
have explained,

the sooner we,
will be allowed,
to enjoy the sun,
and not be cowed.

Heroes Don't Wear Capes

Heroes don't wear capes,
or have some super speed.
They are all the selfless ones,
in our times of need.

Doctors, nurses, healthcare,
who stay at the front line.
Always turning up for work,
each and every time.

Those that keep us fed,
from field to a shop,
and those in the chain,
as deliveries do not stop.

The cleaners and the carers,
often bottom of the pile,
yet they are all still out there,
working all the while.

They must be exhausted,
yet they are there for us.
Taking extra risks,
whilst we stay home and fuss.

As we are stuck at home,
to try and stop the spread.
Let's all try and imagine,
what's in each heroes head.

Our heroes they are human,
and we must all protect,
those who do so very much.
We love you and respect.

I know that we can't hug them,
but we just have to say.
How much we appreciate,
our heroes every day.

You know who the heroes are,
and if these bad times pass,
keep supporting heroes,
as they are total class.

Thank you for reading.

I hope you enjoyed these rhymes. If you did then I'd be very grateful if you could leave a review.

If you want to see more of my work, including fiction then please visit https://alistairbirch.com or follow me on these links:

https://www.facebook.com/alistairbirchauthor

https://twitter.com/ABirchAuthor

You can email me on:
alistairbirchauthor@gmail.com

Acknowledgements

I wanted to finish with a big thank you to my lovely wife Claire whose unwavering support means I got to create this collection. I don't think this poem collection, the thriller, the marathons and all the other things would have happened if you weren't in my life.

I am truly lucky to have you in my corner.

Printed in Great Britain
by Amazon